A Wish upon a Star

Valerie A. Phillips

Illustrated by Linda Umholtz

AuthorHouse™
1663 Liberty Drive
Bloomington, IN 47403
www.authorhouse.com
Phone: 1-800-839-8640

First published by AuthorHouse 11/15/2010

ISBN: 978-1-4520-7712-3 (sc)

Library of Congress Control Number: 2010917185

Printed in the United States of America

This book is printed on acid-free paper.

To my beautiful daughters
and all who wish upon a star.

To my mom and family.

In loving memory of my "Star Pony."

After a long day of moving into their new home, Cara and her mom sat on the porch enjoying the warm spring night.

Looking up at the star-filled sky, Cara's mom said, "Look, honey, a shooting star! Quick, make a wish."

Cara looked up to the sky, closed her eyes tightly, and wished for a horse of her very own. She had always wanted a horse, and now that they had moved to an old farmhouse in the country, she was hoping her parents would get her the horse of her dreams.

Cara awoke the next morning to a knock on her bedroom door.

"Time to get up," said her mom and dad. "Do you want to come with us and explore that old barn in the backyard?"

Cara jumped out of bed and said, "I sure do." She thought about the wish she had made the night before and secretly hoped her parents were about to surprise her with a horse of her own.

When they got to the barn, Cara's dad pulled open the big, creaky door. As the light filtered into the dark barn, it illuminated an unmistakable image. Standing beneath a window amid some old, musty hay was the figure of a carousel horse.

Cara squealed in delight as she ran toward it. "Mom! Dad! Look! Look! It's a carousel horse!" Although Cara was excited, she was still a little disappointed because she had hoped and wished for a real horse. However, when she looked into the eyes of this old, forgotten carousel horse, she knew in her heart that there was something very special and unique about him.

The carousel horse was covered with dust and cobwebs.

Cara ran her hands over the smooth wooden horse, wiping it clean. The horse had lost all of its color with the exception of a few remnants of white and gold paint.

"He is so beautiful. May I keep him?" asked Cara.

Overjoyed with their daughter's happiness, they replied, "Of course, honey."

Every day, Cara spent time out in the old barn playing with the carousel horse. They had endless imaginary adventures where Cara would pretend that they were galloping across the magnificent countryside. Cara loved her carousel horse and the time she spent with him.

As the days passed, Cara noticed that the carousel horse was beginning to look brighter, as if some of his color was returning, and his eyes almost seemed to have a sparkle to them.

One day, Cara went out to the barn only to find that her carousel horse was not under the window where she had left him. In a complete panic, she started to run out of the barn to tell her mom—but then stopped when she heard a soft, playful whinny behind her. Cara slowly turned toward the sound. Her heart began to pound, and her eyes grew wide in amazement, for she could not believe what she was seeing.

There before her stood the carousel horse full of color and life.
His golden mane and tail sparkled, and his white body shimmered.
His bridle and saddle were brilliantly colored and adorned with
sweet flowers, and his big, dark, loving eyes spoke of kindness.

Cara slowly approached him and placed her hand on his shoulder.
His coat felt like satin, and he quivered at her touch.

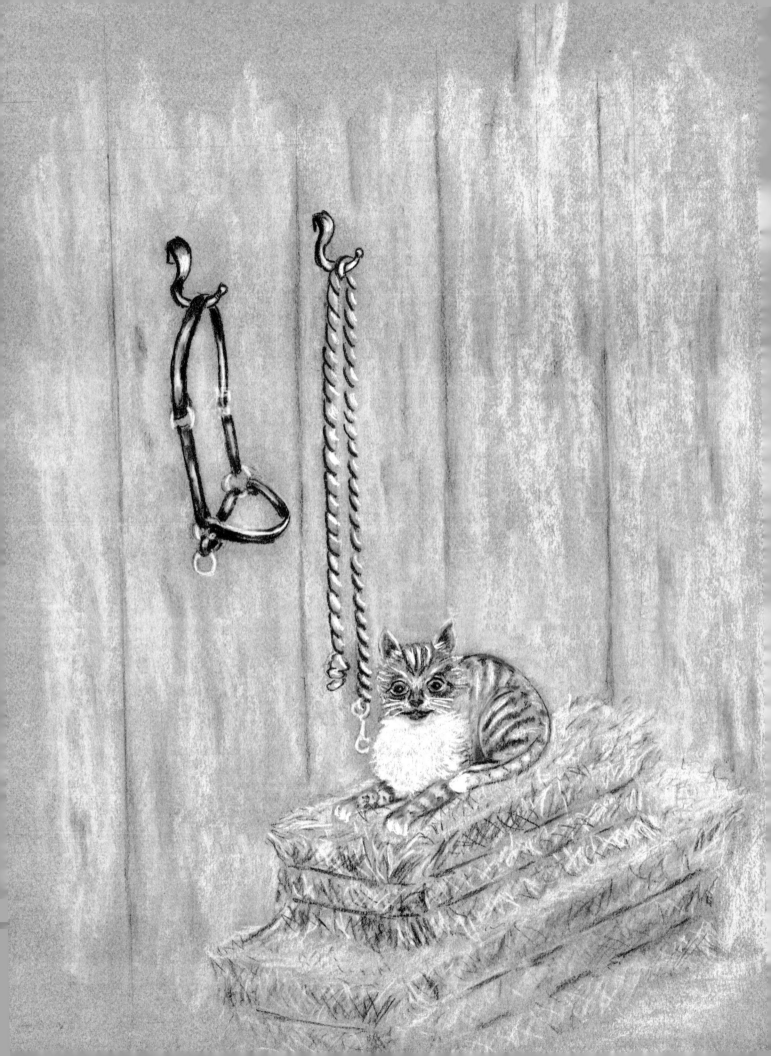

"You're alive!" said Cara.

"Yes, I am alive," replied the carousel horse as he playfully flicked his head in the air. His voice sounded much like Cara's, but she noted a bit of a whinny sound to some of his words. Cara was amazed that he was speaking and giggled at the sound of his voice.

"But how?" said Cara in disbelief.

"It is your love that has brought the life back to me," said the carousel horse. "I was created to bring smiles and laughter to children, yet I have been in this old barn for years. I have longed for my days as a carousel horse. Even though I was chipped and faded, you loved me, and that love has brought the color and life back to me."

"I don't understand how you came to life," said Cara.

"You see," said the carousel horse, "when I was on the merry-go-round at the park, in the evenings after everyone would go home, my fellow carousel horses and I would come to life. We would frolic in the park all night, eagerly awaiting the next day. We would tell one another stories of the girls and boys we met that day. It was the love of the children that gave us life. So you see, Cara, it is your love that has given me life."

Then, at that moment, the carousel horse knelt down. Without hesitation, Cara slipped her foot into the stirrup, wrapped her fingers into his soft and silky mane, and pulled herself up onto the saddle. She took a hold of the reins, and the carousel horse bounded out of the barn door and into the glorious sunlight.

As they galloped across the meadow, Cara could feel the wind in her face. The cool, crisp spring air was invigorating and full of life. Cara was mesmerized by the rhythmic sound of his hooves pounding the earth beneath them. As they galloped faster and faster, Cara let go of the reins, threw her arms out, and laughed joyfully.

With great speed and agility, Cara and the carousel horse approached a large stone wall at the edge of the meadow. Cara took a deep breath, closed her eyes, and held on tightly. The carousel horse rocked back onto his powerful hind legs, and with one great leap, he sprang over the stone wall. There was a moment of silence when they were in the air, and then Cara heard his front hooves hit the ground and they were off again.

As they galloped through the meadow beyond the stone wall, they came upon a field full of horses. There were two beautiful, large horses with a small foal, and they galloped wildly next to them. The thunder of their hooves was tremendous, and Cara felt excited and happy that her dream was coming true. As they bounded down the hill, they parted with the horses and came to a stream. The carousel horse leaped into the water with a great big splash. Cool water sprayed everywhere. Cara was soaking wet and was overjoyed at the freedom she felt.

Night began to fall as they returned home from their adventure. The carousel horse slowed to a walk and then stopped as they approached the barn. Cara leaned forward and wrapped her arms around the carousel horse's neck. Looking up at the stars, she said, "I'm going to name you Star, for it was a star I wished upon and then I found you."

Star's wish also came true. He was alive and loved again, doing what he was created to do—bringing smiles to the faces of children and joy to their hearts.

Cara and Star fell asleep under the beautiful star-filled sky.
They both learned that through the power of love, dreams and
wishes can come true.

LaVergne, TN USA
03 December 2010
207200LV00001B